LOOK AND FIND®

THE BATMAN

™

Illustrated by Art Mawhinney
Written by William Shears
Batman created by Bob Kane

Published by Louis Weber, C.E.O., Publications International, Ltd.
7373 North Cicero Avenue, Lincolnwood, Illinois 60712

Ground Floor, 59 Gloucester Place, London W1U 8JJ

www.pilbooks.com

www.dckids.com

Look and Find is a registered trademark of
Publications International, Ltd.

8 7 6 5 4 3 2 1

ISBN 1-4127-3564-5

Deep beneath the ground under Wayne Manor lies the Batcave. Here Bruce Wayne and his butler Alfred learn of the hideous schemes that Batman's enemies are plotting. Look around for this Batgear to help equip Batman for adventures to come.

Batarang

Batman Polar Armor

Glider Wings

Batcomputer

Jet-Pack

Aquatic Outfit

Ozwald Cobblepot, a.k.a. the Penguin, has taken over the Gotham Zoo. With an army of penguins and other birds at his disposal, Cobblepot plans to wreak havoc on the city — and then the world! Find these feathered fiends before they swoop at Batman.

Cockatoo

Raven

Ostrich

Blue Jay

Eagle

Dodo

Batman's pumped-up archrival Bane is on the loose on the streets of Gotham ... and he's got destruction on his mind. Look for these bewildered bystanders and whisk them to safety.

Scotty Skittlesworth

Polly Pendleton

Ted Terry

Fred Firestein

Wally Warren

Cal Collins

Batman is in for a wild ride. The Joker has taken over an old amusement park. Setting a trap for our hero in this funhouse, the Clown Prince of Crime may have the last laugh. Help Batman find these scary carnival villains before it's too late!

Werewolf

Skeleton

Vampire

Bearded Lady

Clown

Strongman

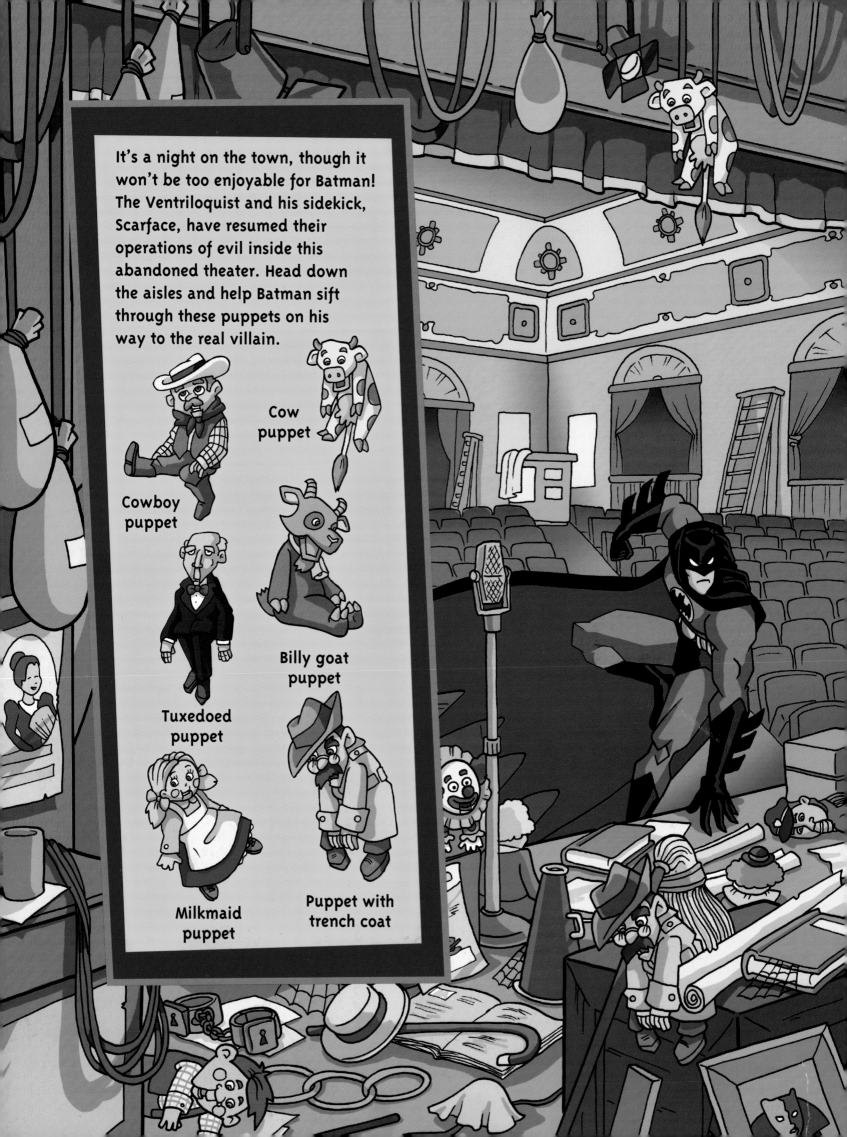

It's a night on the town, though it won't be too enjoyable for Batman! The Ventriloquist and his sidekick, Scarface, have resumed their operations of evil inside this abandoned theater. Head down the aisles and help Batman sift through these puppets on his way to the real villain.

Cow puppet

Cowboy puppet

Tuxedoed puppet

Billy goat puppet

Milkmaid puppet

Puppet with trench coat

Meow! Catwoman has slinked into a pet shop to rob it. As soon as the Dark Knight shows up to trap her, she releases the shop's animals to slow him down. Find these cats to clear the way for Batman to grab this leather-clad burglar.

Calico cat

Siamese cat

A hairless cat

A black cat

Maine Coon cat

A fluffy white cat

Wayne Enterprises is throwing its yearly Winter Charity Gala. Except this year there is an uninvited and unwelcome guest—Mr. Freeze! Find this expensive jewelry before Mr. Freeze gets his chilly claws on it.

Diamond tiara

Large blue gem necklace

Emerald-encrusted women's shoes

A large ruby ring

Gold cufflinks

A silver pocketwatch

Batman has finally locked up every villain at Arkham Asylum—where they belong. After his long battles, the Dark Knight can sleep soundly, since these ne'er-do-wells have been vanquished... or can he? Find these objects that have been smuggled past Arkham's security.

The Joker's laughing lapel flower

The Ventriloquist's dummy, Scarface

Mr. Freeze's freeze-ray gun

The Penguin's monocle

Catwoman's whip

One of Bane's thugs

Spelunk back into the Batcave and find these souvenirs from Batman's previous battles:

- ✓ Newspaper showing a Batman sighting
- ✓ A ripped costume
- ✓ A joker card from the Joker
- ✓ One of Penguin's umbrellas
- ✓ A broken "Scarface" dummy from the Ventriloquist
- ✓ A Catwoman mask
- ✓ Bruce Waine

Return to the Gotham Zoo to find these frigid things:

- ✓ Skis
- ✓ Sock cap
- ✓ Husky dog
- ✓ Mittens
- ✓ Snow shoes
- ✓ Ice skates

Head back to the streets of Gotham to find these city items that were strewn around during Bane's rampage:

- ✓ Newspaper
- ✓ Streetlight
- ✓ Manhole cover
- ✓ Garbage can
- ✓ "Dead end" street sign
- ✓ Pay phone

Sneak back into the Joker's amusement park to find these carnival treats:

- ✓ Baby doll
- ✓ Cotton candy
- ✓ Stuffed-animal monkey
- ✓ Caramel apple
- ✓ Rubber duck
- ✓ Hot dog

Head through the lobby and back into the theater to give Batman a hand at finding these props that were left behind:

- ✓ Magician handcuffs
- ✓ Top hat
- ✓ Poster of a tap-dancer duo
- ✓ Ukulele
- ✓ Blonde, curly wig
- ✓ Old-fashioned microphone

Prowl back to the pet shop and look for these other feline findems:

- ✓ Cat collar
- ✓ Scratching post
- ✓ Cat litter box
- ✓ Can of cat food
- ✓ Catnip
- ✓ Toy mouse

Swing back to the Wayne Winter Charity Gala and defrost these frozen party necessities:

- ✓ Frozen champagne glass
- ✓ Frozen punch bowl
- ✓ Frozen roasted chicken
- ✓ Frozen waiter
- ✓ Frozen flower arrangement
- ✓ Frozen trumpet player

Admit yourself into Arkham Asylum to find these items:

- ✓ Straitjacket
- ✓ Handcuffs
- ✓ Syringe
- ✓ Psychiatrist
- ✓ Stretcher
- ✓ Nurse